In ancient times, Japanese farmers believed the dragonfly was the spirit of the rice plant. Dragonflies were a welcome sign of a good rice harvest. The dragonfly became one of the emblems of the Emperor and was praised in many Japanese poems and songs. Akitsu-shimu – an old name for Japan, means Dragonfly Island.

For Kiyoshi, and those who dare to dream. M.W.

Library of Congress Cataloging-in-Publication Data

Watson, Mary, 1953-
   The paper dragonfly / Mary Watson.
      p. cm.
   Summary: Instead of learning the more practical farming skills his father tries to teach him, Kiyoshi is fascinated by the dragonflies around the rice paddies, which inspires him to craft a lantern that changes his destiny.
   ISBN 0-9726614-3-3 (hardcover : alk. paper)
   [1. Dragonflies--Fiction. 2. Farm life--Fiction. 3. Lanterns--Fiction. 4. Fathers and sons--Fiction.] I. Title.

PZ7.W3278Pap 2007
[E]--dc22
                                        2007016652

The Paper Dragonfly

Mary Watson

Kiyoshi held the moon on a long bamboo pole over the village of Shinshu. The villagers cheered as he lit the night sky with his beautiful lantern. Then his father's voice broke through his dream and the room was dark and it was time for the fieldwork to begin.

Kiyoshi's mother and sisters were already carefully wrapping and tying omochi into bundles for lunch.

"Hurry, Kiyoshi, we must begin planting before the sun is too hot," his father called.

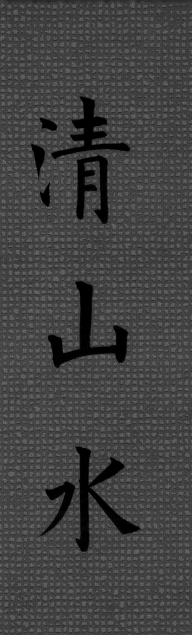

By the time Kiyoshi and his father reached the rice paddy, the sun had spread a golden blanket over the chilly, dark earth. His father cinched up his robe and stepped barefoot into the cold mud.

He carefully took a seedling from his pouch with his middle and index finger and with his thumb pushed its tiny roots into the soft mud.

"Someday," he told Kiyoshi, "this land will be yours and you will grow the rice to feed your family."

But Kiyoshi was listening to the hum of dragonfly wings. He watched as they searched the mud for a place to lay their eggs.

"Push the roots in with your thumb," his father said firmly, reclaiming the boy's attention.

Kiyoshi wanted to please his father but feared he would never make a good farmer. From the time he was a small boy, his only interest was making lanterns. His lanterns were so beautiful that they now hung everywhere in the village.

The wind grew strong, blowing the dragonflies off their course and bending the rows of seedlings Kiyoshi had planted.

"It just takes practice and time," his father said.

And in time the rice paddy shimmered
with rows of green seedlings where thousands
of dragonfly eggs waited to hatch.

One night, Kiyoshi's dreams were filled with the hum dragonflies. In the morning he awoke before the sun.

"It's not a work day. Go back to sleep," his mother whispered.

But Kiyoshi jumped out of bed and spread out his paper to sketch the pictures from his dreams. Then, with a sharp knife, he split long bamboo branches and skinned off their bark, soaking and bending them into shape. Delicately, he covered the bamboo skeleton with fine, translucent rice paper until it became a beautiful dragonfly lantern.

When Kiyoshi presented it to his family, his mother said, "What a splendid lantern you have made! We must save it to hang on our door during the Festival of the New Moon!"

But Kiyoshi's father barely noticed the lantern. "Tomorrow we must return to the field to check our seedlings," he declared. "There will be little to celebrate if the rice does not grow."

By July, dragonfly nymphs were crawling up the long green stems of rice in the rice paddy. "It is a good sign, Kiyoshi. It will be a good harvest," his father said.

Bending over a stem of rice, Kiyoshi examined a young dragonfly. "Where are his wings, Father?"

"They are just hidden because they are wet. When the sun dries his wings, he will fly away."

"Where will he go?" Kiyoshi asked.

"High into the mountains to escape the hot summer," his father said, wiping his brow.

By September, the field was red with dragonflies and the rice was ready for harvesting.

"The Emperor will be pleased," said Kiyoshi's father as they filled the silos. "There will be rice enough for everyone and there will be rice to sell."

月光

The fifteenth day of the new moon was a day of celebration. Everyone swept a fresh path to their door and lit Kiyoshi's lanterns, to thank the gods for the good harvest and to welcome the Emperor. That night the brilliant colored lanterns out shone the moon and stars.

Kiyoshi lit his favorite dragonfly lantern and was hanging it on the door when a strong gust of wind pulled it from his hand.

Down the road it flew, with Kiyoshi's mother and sisters chasing behind.

It landed in a pile of straw, where it burst into flames. The burning straw blew into a nearby field and the fire quickly spread. The villagers raced to the field with buckets of water until the fire was finally out.

Long after the fire was out, dark clouds of smoke billowed up from the smoldering field.

"Oh Mother," Kiyoshi cried, "I never should have made the lantern!"

Kiyoshi's mother saw her son's great despair but could not comfort him.

Just at that moment, the Emperor's soldiers galloped into the smoke-filled village with great speed and excitement. "The Emperor spotted your fire from on top of the hill!" they announced.

The Emperor arrived shortly in a gold trimmed carriage lined with silk. He stepped down into the street, coughing and squinting in the smoke.

"“Who made these lanterns?” he bellowed, gaping at the countless lanterns that lined the village streets.

Kiyoshi stepped forward, trembling with shame. “It is I, your Holiness,” he confessed. “It was my lantern that started the fire....”

The Emperor did not respond. He just paraded down the street followed by his legion of soldiers.

The villagers waited in silence until finally, he returned from his inspection.

"Where is your father?" the Emperor asked Kiyoshi.

When Kiyoshi's father stepped forward, he was astonished by the Emperor's words.

"It is only fitting that the palace of the Emperor be lit with the finest lanterns in all the land. Therefore, with your permission, I shall appoint your son Official Lantern Maker of the Imperial Palace."